There are distinct differences between him and her.

1

him

tw: this book may trigger anyone who has experienced suicidal thoughts, rape/sexual assault, eating disorders etc.

Its time for a new one.

Never in my life did I believe anyone was capable of hurting me again.

I told you any and everything there was to know.

Every flaw, insecurity and trauma.

So why did you still choose to add to it?

-   why destroy what you begged for?

Im teaching myself to stop romanticizing every happy moment.

Not everyone is someone and not every dream is reality.

Some things are just life fillers.

I may be a lost cause

- please don't waste your time trying to
  save me

I always seem to ignore the truth for some temporary sense of happiness

But are we really happy lying to ourselves?

Creativity creates us

Creates this

Creates

We

Create

To be in touch with your inner demon is to know what you are choosing is going to hurt you, but nothing can stop you anyway.

- Impulse control

Love doesn't just sit there like a stone

It has to be tended to like a garden, remove the weeds and water the regrowth.

- Nurture me

What is beautiful?

Is it the way I break down at the smallest thing into spiraling anxiety?

Maybe it's the way I look at the floor so you can't see me smile?

But I know for sure it isn't me you're talking about

Not really me anyway

Because then you wouldn't be saying beautiful

More like beautiful mess
Beautiful but broken.

If I ever disappear just know I'm okay
I love you
But I do this

I run away.

Be my peace when my head is in shambles
But
Also be my peace when everything is okay

And all this talk of making love

It's the craving I cannot fix

The addiction I cannot kick

I want to experience this

I need it.

The sensation I feel from our sensations is sensational.

Come ride this high you have me on for I may
never feel like this again.

Paint me the picture in your mind you get
when I come to mind.

don't be afraid, there's no way it's worse than
mine.

I yearn for a relationship, friendship, that will give me some substance. Something for me to hold on to.

I'm tired of pouring and pouring and never being refilled.

I told you I was delicate like a flower

Instead of taking that and listening, you picked every single petal off until I was weaker than I was before you.

- I guess maybe there were no petals to begin with.

I could give you the whole world, but you'd want the fucking universe.

You have made me question every compliment someone gives me.

Made me think no one will be able to appreciate me because of flaws you decided I have.

Had me out here thinking I am less than and accepting it because you told me no one else would put up with me and truly love me.

That's not what love is.

Its crazy too because I hadn't realized how
tight you had me wrapped around your finger.

How stupid of me to play into this for so long.

To the readers of this:

I wish I could help you understand exactly what I mean by all of this. I wish for own sanity that no one can relate to this. But, if anyone does, I am so sorry and I hope this helps you in some way.

Don't ever think I'll need you again.

You said "you'd go crazy without me" one too many times.

Eat your words and watch this.

I remember the day
           I fell
                 Like it was yesterday.

  -   Got up now though

Got a cup half full of my love

Half full of my fear.

To be able to understand me is to be able to walk on water.

The sky and me

We're connected you see

What I can't find the words to share

It will paint for me.

In a world where everything is crazy, and nothing makes sense can you please. Bring me peace?

How am I everything you want and everything you don't?

Is it just who I am?

That makes you want to yell at me every time I say something you don't like?

You convinced me that you were the best for
me

Made me feel awful if ever disagreed.

But it turns out you could not love me the way
I need to be loved.

-   Impossible.

You talk to me as if I am disposable when I am
in fact irreplaceable.

So, watch your mouth

Every once in a while, the world will feel like it's going to stop.

When you meet eyes with someone
                                    You love.

I tend to accept whatever form of love is given to me.

Rather than asking for what I want or what I probably deserve.

I fear that people will think I am asking for too much.

Working on my dependency.

Learning how to depend on myself even
though there's no stability.

I don't fucking want small talk.

Tell me why you flinch at certain words.

Tell me about the things you fear.

Help me understand how to nurture you.

Tell me the ugly so I can tell you it's beautiful.

I want to love you.

Let me.

Hold the parts of me no one has seen.

Trauma, it's one of those things I am familiar with.
Bittersweet.

Mostly bitter

Kind of overwhelming.

But I won't let it consume me.

- Not this time

Bright like the sun

My plants grow for you.

Be careful,

Some days I am just going to be very sad with no understandable explanation.

I'm sorry, it's me.

Love overwhelms me.

Please do not disturb my being if you are just
going to break my heart.

I deserve to eat. I deserve to

I can drive to you, get high with you. Spend
time with you, and you still don't pick me.
I never wanted to be on of those pick me girls,
but I don't understand why it's so hard to pick
me.

Fuck.

I never realized how much trauma I have
experienced.

No wonder you don't want me I don't blame
you.

8 years ago, you took away my choice.
I have never put this to words because you
told me not to.
I screamed once, you punished me for that.
I am weak.
I feel guilty,
For not trying harder to have the choice.
And now the scars last forever.

"you know you wanted it"
"stop trying to blame me you were teasing me"
"if you tell anyone ill fucking shoot you"
"I mean look how you dress what did you expect"
"you said you wanted me why won't you have sex with me"
"you gotta chill I didn't force you"
"are you really gonna lie and say you didn't start it"
"shut the fuck up"

You're irritated by my existence.
You call me annoying to the point where I
apologize for my normalcy,
In fear of being annoying to anyone in life but
in reality,
I don't need to be sorry to you.
I am only sorry you couldn't see me for me.

The shame I feel in saying no.

It doesn't even feel like I have the option to not want anything.

Remember when you told me because you bought me flowers and took me out that you expected to have sex with me so it was weird that I wouldn't?

I guess it was later no surprise two years later when he touched me you called me a whore and said it was my fault.

You killed the romantic in me and I'm literally and author of love poems.

Fear of rejection leaves you rejected.

Fear of abandonment leaves you abandoned.

- I cling so hard that my fears come true.

In case you ever wondered what started this.

You told me one time your preference in a woman's body.

I tried so hard to become that, to get thick.

That eventually I hated myself and forced myself into disordered eating to lose it all.

It's been over a year and I hate food and I hate my body.

You throw in my face times I hurt you months
ago in a time when we're in love to wound me.

Why?

If I give you love you pull and if I don't you
cling.
i'm afraid i've met me.

I hate blaming you for all of this. I feel so guilty, I didn't want it to be this way but the scars you left are so permanent I have to blame you.

- Its literally your fault.

How could you break what you wanted in the first place?

Screaming and fighting and cursing me out is just not love.

How dare you convince me that was passion when really you can't control your own emotions, so you manipulate mine.

The things you say to me in anger will replay in my thoughts for a million lifetimes.

I gave up. Finally.

I'm ending this self-harm cycle you lost your vice.

In between

Mastering detachment because I keep
attaching myself to people, things, feelings

And I'll always be let down. Let things come
and go freely its less detrimental to your soul.

I feel as though my qualities are a burden.

I feel annoying, complicated, hard to love, I wish I didn't exist this way or just maybe as someone else.

- it's really lonely in my mind

Ive been told if my mental wasn't so
fucked up people would date me.

Fuck that im worthy of love regardless.

It's taking a lot of mental healing and true intention to even erase this level of hurt.

Certain words make me flinch

Finding that one of my biggest triggers is people leaving.

Not in the literal leaving my life, but more so walking away, ignoring me, ending a conversation and not finishing talking.

I don't like to feel as though at the drop of a hat a person could leave.

- fight or flight

I have dreamt my life will repeat itself

It is a constant battle between me and my
thoughts

There is too much trauma there for me to
allow my thoughts to manifest into reality
again.

Let me show you

At 3 am that day I stood in front of my door to stop you from leaving. Tears down my face just asking you to finish our conversation.

You laughed at me and screamed to stop crying and when I wouldn't move out of your way you moved me aggressively.

- Don't get in peoples' way, noted.

I think certain people only want to be in your life when you are alone. They won't be around when you are full of life only when are in the dark so that they can feed their ego by thinking they're helping you.

I can't decide what I look like in the mirror

Body dysmorphia is kicking my ass and I cannot keep blaming people for how I picture my body.

Her.

This is the most overwhelming love ever.

All consuming, constant, and so so intense.

The person who everyone knew me to be does not exist.

I used to feel shame in this.

Feared that I was less than because of what people said.

But you changed my life forever and I never want any other love.

Something similar to love at first sight...

And something like feeling like I've known you
forever

You're soft, delicate and sweet I just want to cater to you in every way.

I hate affection and you turned my love
language in physical touch.

Sliding my hand up the side of your body

Holding eye contact while you touch me

Waking up next to you

- Just a few of my favorite views.

Being shown that there are other ways to be loved is an interesting experience.

I thought the game we used to play was the only way anyone could love me.

I was head over heels for this one.

June 2.

You took this relationship and made it nothing
to you and I haven't breathed the same since.

Not only did you change the way I viewed how this is all supposed to go but you showed me what it is I want, while it is not you, I thank you anyway.

I feel like the cycle of asking "why not me" ends with you.

I had to look in the mirror and convince myself that I am not lesser than because you chose to dispose of me.

Her is not actually that much different from him.

You used me and toyed with me, and it hurt worse because you didn't have to do it like that, I would've understood.

I need to live in someone else's brain its way too hard to breathe in here.

Red flag 1:

You told me you were a serial cheater and I overlooked it

This time, I thought okay you get anxious too
maybe she won't make me feel like I don't
exist for feeling this way.

- wrong

Red flag 2:

Told me you loved me after 2 weeks

-    maybe lesbian stereotypes are true...

Something about someone as beautiful as you breaking my heart over and over again made it worth it to me.

You looked so good while you lied to me

"atleast she didn't cheat, she left first"

I used to think to myself, but you probably did that too and I didn't realize until now how many signs were there that I missed.

Red flag 3:

College basketball. Friends with ex.

I heard that your first heartbreak with a woman hurts more than with a guy and I didn't understand how the gravity was different

 until I felt like I was sinking for 6 months because of you.

The night of that stupid ass phone call I knew
you were just as bad as any guy could ever be.

Does she know it was me you were on the
phone with when she walked in?

Red flag 4:

Can't communicate her emotions.

You were the first girl I fell in love with and admitted it to the world.

The first girl I let touch me, like really touch me.

-   Fuck you for having that first be bitter.

You became my everything and you saying all this now makes my throat burn.

How could you expect me to not need you?
When all you've done is be there for me for
over a year, like yes in crisis I will reach out to
you like its normal you can't expect this habit
to change so quickly.

How am I making it worse by asking for your
help? You're the one who allowed me to be
codependent.

You're the one that fell out of love not me so why do I feel like I've done something wrong?

I had to beg you to be there for me, support me. Literally pull teeth trying to get even a bare minimum out of you.

- Funny I thought this was end all be all.

Red flag 5:

Tall. Pretty. Curly hair.

Your friends said you were that nigga for being with me, I had to convince people you were different so they wouldn't clown me for being with you.

- You're dumb for fucking that up

You were supposed to be the one that saved me, but I saved you and you left me out in the dark one day like you got what you wanted and left.

Only this want wasn't even sexual you wanted to be healed so you broke me.

You taught me how to value myself. Although you did not yourself value me,

I was given a choice to stay and allow or leave and not have to endure anymore.

And for the first (actual) time

I chose me.

Toxic masculinity runs in your masculine energy, and you have never felt safe enough to let your feminine energy be more prominent so instead you act like a dick and cause others to feel their femininity being tampered and feel that they cannot be vulnerable anymore.

No, these girls are not "turning into you" you're affecting their energy display.

- Leave her alone you aren't even good for her

Reflecting on who I was a year ago I just want to say thank you for the pain.

In the end they hurt the same

and you realize there is no real difference
between him and her

you just have to pick who want to endure the
difficult parts with.

Dear Reader,

Thank you so much for reading ☺☺☺☺☺☺☺

This piece means so much to me. I wrote this starting in jan of 2020, pre covid and finished around sept 2021 so the timeline is very broad.

If you or anyone you know have felt any of this before, im sorry, I love you and im grateful this made it to you.

- Chloe

Made in the USA
Middletown, DE
30 August 2023